KAPPIYA'S STORY COLLECTIONS-1

KAPPIYA CLASSICS

Contents

ONE

1. *Peach Blossom Luck* by *Kow Shih Li*

The three of us sat in the fortune teller's office, an eight by ten space tucked at the back of a tailor's shop. The glass front overlooked bales of cloth in various shades of grey, blue and black. Apart from the view, it was surprisingly businesslike. I had expected at least some incense, the sundry deities or feng shui diagrams but there were none in sight.

I sat in the fabric covered chair, the type clerks used in administrative offices. Connie wassubdued and I assumed that she had stopped crying. I could not see past those oversized, opaque Jackie-O sunglasses she had on. In the car, she had cried all the way here, big sobbing breaths, between which she gasped out her account of how she had struggled to support her truant husband in his younger days. I heard for the sixth time how she had to take the bus to work so that he could use the money saved for her car to start his now successful trading business. Her crying invariably took on a slightly high pitched whine when she said, as she always did, "How could he do this to me? After all that I've done for him, how could he leave me for a twenty year old cheap trick?"

The "cheap trick", according to Datin Tai, one of our regular lunch friends, was a part time caddie at the golf club where Connie's husband plays. Pretty face and nice legs, but of course we never said that in Connie's presence.

The fortune teller cleared his throat. He was a short man in a slightly grimy Pagoda T-shirt tucked into polyester trousers that were probably made by the tailor out front. His face was smooth, shiny and impersonal. With more hair, it would have been difficult to place his age.

"Who wants to 'see' life fortune?" he said in Cantonese, nodding questioningly at Connie and me. That was the reason I was here. Connie needed a translator, and the rest of the lunch gang needed an inside account of what was soon to transpire.

I indicated Connie and told him about her predicament. I had never been very good with details and it took me less time to tell it than one of those commercials on radio.

"Datin Tai recommended you," I said, after I was done narrating the facts in what I thought was adequate detail. "You remember, Datin Tai from Damansara? She said you helped her when she had this same type of problem two years ago."

Datin Tai had told us in great detail, over a 3-hour sushi lunch, how this fortune teller had saved her husband from the clutches of a "gold-digging GRO from hell". There were readings and talismans given to hide around the home. She was convinced that her husband saw the error of his ways soon after, and even became a more successful businessman from that point onwards. Connie was skeptical but on the verge of desperation. I imagined her grasping at the talisman straws offered by Datin Tai.

The fortune teller asked for Connie's time, date and year of birth. We had come fully prepared. We had hers and her husband's printed on Connie's company letterhead paper. It was the Chinese date of birth that was required and Connie had spent two days getting her office staff run a search for a conversion calendar on the Internet.

Eighty ringgit per reading, we were told. One hundred and fifty ringgit to include a reading for Connie's husband. A ten ringgit discount for a two-in-one. Extra charges for other things. Datin Tai's talismans must have been one of those optional, cryptic other things.

On the fortune teller's table was a tray with two stacks of pre-printed forms - pink and blue. He pulled out a pink one. It had the crisscrossed Chinese character for female in one corner. I presumed the blue would be for men. The paper was neatly printed like a job application form, with blank spaces, ruled lines and little headers. The Pagoda T-shirt was the only incongruity that belied his professionalism, I thought to myself.

I wondered if Connie noticed any of this. She sat in the way she always did when we were out for tea - legs neatly crossed at the knee, hands on the handbag cradled in her lap. Today, she had her new monogrammed Louis Vuitton. "I bought it to cheer myself up," she had said on one of those days when she wore her brave, smiling face. If she had a tall glass of iced coffee in front

of her, she would have looked perfectly normal to anyone who knew her.

Connie was a good looking woman. Not beautiful or even pretty, but she had a polish to her that obscured all physical flaws. A polish honed and developed by years of carefully studying and assimilating the habits of the very rich. She wore a sheen buffed to perfection by money. Her husband was wealthy enough to have no need of the titles bestowed by local royalty, which implied that he was richer by far than Datin Tai's husband.

I turned to the fortune teller. He had started muttering, his fingers twitched. His left thumb touched each of the other fingers on the same hand in turn. The ballpoint pen in his right flew over the pink sheet, a number here, a word there. The blank spaces were filling up. Connie's fate was being calculated and summarized, like an answer to a math exam question.

I reached out and held Connie's hand. She smiled and two black rivulets appeared under her dark glasses. Her tears were making her mascara run again. A grey drop dislodged from her chin and made a tiny splash on her bag. I wriggled my fingers over my face to tell her. She said, "Oh," and "Oh, oh" when she saw the smudge on her bag. She dabbed a tissue at the bag before wiping her tears.

The fortune teller was now poring over a red-covered book with newsprint pages. It looked like a cheap dictionary. This, I recognized. It was the Tong Shu. One edition is published every year, chronicling life and fate based on the simple statistic of date and time of birth. Anyone who knew this basic information would be able to have his life laid out year by year, like a lifetime horoscope. A destiny which completely disregards all other variables and social indicators like education, upbringing, social status or geographical location. If the Tong Shu says you will marry at sixteen, it would happen irregardless of whether you were born Chinese or Icelandic. I wondered if Connie's reading would be accurate.

The fortune teller closed the book and put down his pen. There was an air of finality when he smoothed the pink form with his hands. I sat straighter, ready to do my duty. I had to make sure that Connie understood everything that he was about to say. Datin Tai had reminded me not to forget any detail. She and the rest would be all ears at our lunch tomorrow and I was to relate all the juicy bits accurately.

"I have calculated both yours and your husband's lives. Your life is quite good, actually but hard. I can see a lot of work. You must work at everything. Work for money, work for health, even work to get love husband. Nothing comes easy to you."

He went on to say that her parents had died when she was eight and described how she had to work to put herself through school. I made mental notes of everything.

"Twenty two years old, you got married. Your husband was rich and you made him richer. You bring a lot of good luck to him." I repeated everything in English.

I imagined Datin Tai asking me, "Are you sure that was what he said? Did he say she made him richer or she made him rich? I thought they were poor when they started off. You know, that story about money for the car?"

Connie was listening to me, nodding and sniffling a little at the same time. The crumpled tissues were piling up on the table. I felt sorry for her. It was strange feeling. I was more used to being envious of her perfect, wealthy life.

"Now, your husband is complicated. He is heaven born with 'dou fa wan', the peach blossom luck. The playboy luck. Throughout his whole life, he will have women coming and going but three times he will encounter real interference, serious relationship."

I repeated this. Connie said, "Three times? So what am I supposed to do? How do I change his luck, break this thing? Ask him if there is something he can give me."

After a translation delay, like a badly edited movie, the fortune teller replied, "You cannot change his luck. Only he can change if he wants to."

"But he doesn't want to. He wants to divorce my friend here and marry this other girl."

The fortune teller took off his rimless glasses, put them on the table and sighed. Up until this point, he had been talking to me. Now he looked directly at Connie. He said, "Please translate this question for your friend. 'Didn't your husband divorce his first wife to marry you?' "

We drove home in silence that afternoon.

2. <u>*Of Mother and Daughter*</u> by *Noby*

Tina pedaled home excitedly. In her schoolbag was the letter from the State Sports Council explaining that she had been selected to represent her state in the coming Malaysian Schools Sports Meet (MSSM) in Kuala Lumpur. Held each year, the MSSM was the culmination of all sporting meets throughout the year starting from schools, districts and states level. At the MSSM, participants were selected school children from all the 14 states of

Malaysia representing the states where their schools were. And Tina had been selected to represent her state, Terengganu, in athletics, running her pet events, 400meters, 800meters and the 4x400meters relay. Her selection was announced proudly by the school headmaster during the school assembly that morning. Only two students were selected from her school. Tina for the under 16 category and a boy for the under 18. Tina re-savoured the feeling when her name was announced. She felt as though she was on cloud nine. The announcement was totally unexpected. Tina recalled heads turning in her directions. Eyes looking at her with admirations, perhaps with envy too. But Tina did not notice the latter. She only noticed the admirations. She floated around with pride the entire school hours. Friends and teachers kept congratulating and encouraging her. Teachers were especially proud of her for she also excelled in studies, being consistently among the top three best students of her forms. She could not wait to go home to tell her parents. To get her father to sign the letter of consent. Without that she would not be able to go to Kuala Lumpur even though selected.

Half her mind kept dreaming of the excitement of running in MSSM, of going to Kuala Lumpur, the Malaysian Capital City. The other half kept reminding her to pay attention to the road. 'You don't want anything untoward to happen now, do you?' She chided herself. Her skinny suntanned legs pedaled the bicycle furiously. She did not feel the burn of the sun nor the distance. It was 14 km to and from her house to the school. Perhaps pedaling the distance everyday, rain or shine, developed her aptitude and stamina for long distance running. It certainly did not occur to Tina that it was far. It was just something she had to do. And she enjoyed doing it. There was no school bus or public bus plying the road from her village to the school anyway. Her village was that remote. The only alternative was to take the boat downriver to town, walk to the bus station, and then the bus to school. She did this before, and ended up arriving home almost 4 PM everyday when the school dismissed at 1 o'clock. And when she had her sports practices, she sometimes missed the last boat home. On those occasions, she had to cry her heart out before some kindly boatmen took pity on her and sent her back. And to a very unpleasant reception from her mother.

Through her excitement, Tina felt a twinge of worry. Her mother. What would be her reaction? Her mother had always opposed to her sporting activities. Any activity, for that matter, other than staying at home. Her mother belonged to the old school which believed a girl should be at home doing all the girlish things, what ever they were, grimaced Tina. She particularly objected to Tina's wearing those very short shorts when running. She even objected to girls wearing pants. Tina remembered one occasion when her elder sister came home from her boarding school in Seremban. She brought home a couple of friends. One day they decided to go to a picnic at one of the beautiful white sandy beaches in Terengganu. Her sister's friends were from Kuala Lumpur. They dressed themselves in t-shirts and jeans appropriate for a day at the beach. Tina's sister did likewise but in a more loose and baggy pants. Suddenly, her sister burst into the room she shared with Tina, crying.

"Mother wouldn't let me wear the pants, she insists I wear a sarong!" she wailed, worried that she would appear like a real gawky, dummy kampong girl besides her sophisticated city friends.

Tina looked at her with exasperation. "Just go ahead and wear the pants, don't bother with mother," she said. "She will never let you do anything, so you just take the matter into your own hands." Tina's principle of doing things her mother didn't like frequently resulted her receiving the wrong end of the stick.

In fact her mother did not even approve of the picnic but acquiesced only because of her sister's Kuala Lumpur friends. Her more 'yes-mother' sister decided to adopt Tina's principle on that particular occasion, and went off stubbornly with her friends in her baggy pants much to mother's ire.

During that time, her mother was giving Tina a complete cold shoulder. Tina had kept her silence and distance as usual. She was used to her mother's cold treatment. It always happened during the second term of school when the sports season started. Tina would be late home almost every day and sometimes even during the weekends taking parts in various sports activities and this upset her mother to no end. And as usual Tina never paid any attention to her mother's objections. She never could understand nor accept her mother's opposition to her involvement in sports. However, that time it was more serious. Mother had not talked to Tina for almost two months other than the occasional grumpy 'ump' or 'hah' to Tina's efforts at reconciliation.

It had started with the spike shoes incident two months earlier. Tina had just come back from school in the afternoon and so had her father. They were having lunch together, seated on the floor, around a large tray containing an assortment of dishes prepared by her mother. Her mother was hovering around ensuring her father had everything to his liking.

Suddenly Tina asked her father,' Father, can you buy me a pair of spike shoes?'

Tina had always dreamed of owning a pair of spike shoes for running because she had been running bare foot, even when representing her school or district.. Tina visualized herself in her Adidas running attire complete with golden Adidas spikes shoes, looking like her idols, Marina Chin and Junaidah Aman, the two famous Malaysian national runners at that time. The walls of her room were fully covered with pasted newspaper cuttings of these two ladies in various sporting poses before her mother tore them down. The sight of those girls dressed in skimpy running entire was too much for her. She was convinced that they were evil influence on her stubborn daughter. That incidence triggered another cold war between Tina and her mother, as Tina, sulked and sobbed over the torn pictures of her idols.

Her school had a few pairs of spikes but for some reason the sports teacher never lend them to Tina. But Tina's close friend enjoyed the benefit and Tina secretly felt that favouritism was in play. Tina's friend was the daughter of a well respected lawyer and in those days in small town like Tina's, lawyers were like the local dignitaries. She came to school chauffeur driven in a Mercedes car and alighted right at the school corridor instead of the school gate like every one else. On top of that Tina's friend was very pretty and always had an air of a lady about her. Probably because of her upbringing. She was very smart too and very friendly. So everybody including the teachers liked and in awe of her. Compared to her, Tina felt like a rough, gawky kampong girl.

'How much do they cost?" Tina's father asked.

Tina did not get to answer and her father was stunned into silence. Because as soon as her father asked the question, her mother ran out screaming like crazy and slammed the kitchen door with such force that the wooden house trembled. The outburst shocked both Tina and her father. Both made a pretense of continuing their lunch in silence and that was the end of the spike shoes and the beginning of her mother's boycott of Tina. Tina retired to her room to hide her hurt. She was bewildered over her mother's reaction.

Father didn't say he was going to buy me the shoes, right? He was just asking the price. That doesn't mean he was going to buy them for me. Tina went over and over in her mind. She could not understand what was so wrong about her interest in sports.

The teachers encouraged students to be active, right?, so long as you don't neglect your studies. It certainly did not interfere with my studies. Tina thought petulantly.

Tina recalled during the recent school sports day when she emerged as the best Sports Girl for under 16 category. She stopped at a friend's house before going home. A cousin of her friend had won something during the sports day and Tina saw how the family rejoiced and was very proud of him. They made so much noise and such a do about his winning. At that moment Tina wallowed in self-pity because nobody in her family ever showed such pride over her achievements, especially in sports. She did not even dare show any of the medals and trophies that she won for fear of adding more fuel to fire with her mother. When everyone was asleep at night, She would quietly slip her medals and trophies alongside her brother's in the display cabinet in the middle of the house.

'Oo-oo-mph!' the sound of a lorry horn jolted Tina out of her miserable recollections. She was on a bridge and had strayed to the middle. She quickly swerved back to the side sticking her tongue out to the lorry driver for giving her a rude gesture. The lorry passed her with a roar. She started paying more attention to the road. She was nearing home now anyway. After the bridge, she turned right, off the busy main road onto the red gravel road of her village. Her house was just about two kilometers from the junction. On the quiet village road, her mind inadvertantly revert back to her problem. She tried to keep up her confidence. *Surely father would sign the consent letter. He was a teacher himself, was he not? And teachers always encouraged sports right so long as you don't neglect your studies. No one could ever accuse me of that!* Tina tried to comfort herself. Her father was a religious teacher but he was teaching in a regular school not a religious one. *Surely he would understand. Surely he would be proud of my achievement,* Tina assured herself albeit worriedly.

She turned onto the padi field bund that served as the road to her house, bumping and wobbling over the uneven surface of the bund all the way home.

Her father's Honda was parked under the house. So her father was already home. Her heart thudding and hands clammy with cold despite the afternoon heat, Tina went up the stairs and saw her father having lunch with her mother fussing over him as usual. Tina dropped her bag in her room and went to join her father for lunch. No one invited her but she helped herself to a plate and sat herself on the floor in front of the tray. Her mother pointedly ignored her and her father being a man of few words never did say anything. The obstinate side of Tina wished she could just leave without having lunch, but she was hungry and thirsty after all the pedaling in the hot sun. So feeling very small and insecure she swallowed her pride and helped herself to the food. Throughout lunch, her mind was a busy bee, trying to find an opening to tell her father of her happy news. But her mother was always there and she did not have the gut to face a repeat of the dramatic 'Spike Shoes Scene', as she secretly labeled the incident.

Her father retired to his room after lunch. Tina was left mooning about with her problem. How ironic she thought. What would be a very happy news to other people, was such a big problem for her. She curled herself up at her favourite mooning place, at the base of the big *jambu arang* tree, on the fringe of the ripening padi fields at the bottom of her house compound. The soft cool afternoon breeze lulled her to sleep temporarily giving her mind a respite from her problem. She was awakened by the sound of her father's motorbike starting.

She jumped up dismayed. 'Oh no, he's going off, and I have not told him.'

She rushed to the house and was relieved to see her father was only doing the routine check on his motorcycle. Her mother was not in sight. Tina saw her opportunity and, with her heart beat wildly, she approached her father under the house. She squatted beside him.

"Father, I...I...have been chosen to represent Terengganu in M..M..MSS.ssM," Tina stammered. "C...can I go father?' She asked in a small voice. "Teacher said you have to sign a letter if y..you allow m..me go."

Her father turned to look at her. For one brief moment, Tina thought she caught a glimpse of pride in her father's eyes. Then he turned away to continue to tend to his bike without saying a word. Tina was almost in tears.

"You have to ask your mother's permission," she heard her father said softly without looking at her.

Tina's heart almost stopped with disappointment.

How could he ask me to do that when he knows for sure what the answer will be? her painful heart ranted. Tina did not say a word but looked at her father pleadingly for understanding. But he steadfastly looked at his motorcycle.

Tina got up and turned to go up the stairs slowly, shoulders drooping. In the house, she saw her mother sitting on her praying mat. Not one to give up easily, She sat herself on the floor behind her mother waiting for her to finish her prayer and prepared herself for her mother's reaction when she asked her permission. She could not for the life of her think of the possibility of her mother saying yes, but she had to try for she wanted to go to MSSM more than anything else. Oh, maybe as much as she wanted the spike shoes. Her mother finished her prayer and Tina crept nearer. She popped the question timidly then braced herself. Minutes passed nothing happened. It was as though Tina had not spoken. Her mother completely ignored her. Not giving up, Tina waited then asked again. Still her mother did not respond but calmly removed her praying robe and walked away from her. Her mother's snub cut Tina to the quick. She sat there staring at her mother's back forlornly tears rolling down her cheeks.

Tina hid herself in her room sobbing recalling the proud moment in the morning in school, the pride she felt and the admiration she received. Well none of that on the home front, she thought bitterly. She felt bitter about her father too. 'He should make the decision, he is the head of the family, isn't he? Why does he always give in to mother,?' Her vicious thoughts went on and on until finally exhausted she fell asleep forgoing her dinner.

Two days passed. Tina was still no nearer her wish. The next day was the last day for her to submit the consent letter. She grew desperate. She had been going about the house for the past two days with her face hanging down to her knees, skipping most of her meals for she completely lost her appetite. Just as well it was over the weekend so she did not have to attend school. She was not confident of putting up a brave and cheerful front as though everything was alright. But tomorrow, school started again and she had to submit the letter otherwise she would be dropped from the state team. Tears welled up in her eyes again. It was already night and she was seated away from her other siblings who were engrossed in play. She had been doing that ever since the day she asked for the permission. Day time she would hide herself at the base of the *jambu arang* tree and at night she just sat in a corner by herself nursing her disappointment and desperation.

She thought she would give her father another try when suddenly he called to her, *"Where's the letter that I have to sign?"* Tina's heart jumped with joy. The swift shining change to her face brought tears to her father's eyes and he turned away to hide them but Tina never noticed them. Being a child she did not understand her father's dilemma of pleasing his extremely conservative wife and his extremely adventurous, athletic daughter. But Tina was right, being a schoolteacher, he understood. Oblivious to all these, Tina jumped to her feet with such alacrity that she almost stepped over her little sister crawling on the floor nearby. She rushed to her room for the letter and brought it to her father, her hand shaking in her eagerness. As her father signed the letter consenting her to participate, she glanced at her mother sitting away in stony silence. She felt guilty but was too selfish in her joy to let it affect her.

Oh she will come around eventually. Doesn't she always? Tina consoled herself.

3. <u>*Twelve and not stupid*</u>*by Zuraidah Omar*

Papa is late again. It has been two hours since school ended and I feel so foolish, standing here in my school uniform, in front of Kong's Mini-Market. This is where I wait for Papa to pick me up after school; it is just across from the road that goes down to the school. Papa is often late but not as late as this. People entering the shop glance at me, standing here by the entrance with my school-bag tucked between my feet. They appear surprised to see me, still standing here, when they leave the shop. Mr Kong, who is already familiar at the sight of me standing and waiting outside his shop, has a look on his face that seems to say, "Poor girl. Where on earth is her father? How can he leave her waiting for so long?"

I see his car coming up the road and I feel so relieved. For a while, I did think that he had forgotten to pick me up. It did happen once. By the time he came to get me, it was almost evening and I was already in tears. Mama had been out with her friends and was worried to find me not home when she got back. She had then called Papa. If only Mama could drive me to and from school, life would be so much easier for me. She does have a driver's licence and used to drive when we lived in Seremban. But that was so long ago and we now live in KL. She doesn't like driving in KL where people, she says, drive like maniacs.

Papa's car slows down as it comes up to Kong's Mini-Market. It stops and I am just about to jump into the front seat when I notice that there is somebody already there, a woman whom I don't recognise. She looks about the same age as Mama and her skin is as fair as Mama's, except that Mama is Malay and this woman is Chinese. Her long hair is tied in a bun and she wears glasses. I get into the back seat of the car and she turns to smile at me. "Hello Sasha," she says in a rather sweet voice. "I am Auntie May." I am surprised that she knows my name because I know for certain that I've not met her before.

As I am not saying a word and must be staring hard at her, Papa looks at me through the rearview mirror and says, "Don't be rude, Sasha. *Salam* Auntie May." She extends her hands to me in between the two front seats and I take them in mine. She turns to face the front as Papa drives off and I am left looking at the back of their heads as they talk to one another in low voices. I feel confused as they appear to know one another well, but then Papa and Mama, both very sociable people who like going out to parties, have many friends and Auntie May must be one of them.

When Papa and Mama go out to a party, they look very striking indeed. Papa is an attractive man, with thick wavy hair and his eyebrows are also thick. He dresses smartly, coordinating his long-sleeved batik shirt, pants, socks and shoes very well. Mama is almost as tall as Papa and, with her slim figure, she looks good in anything she wears. Her hair is dark and long and she wears it in a bun, just like Auntie May.

Waiting for Papa and having to stand for so long has made me tired, and I can feel myself dozing off. The slow rocking of the car as Papa makes his way through the busy KL traffic lulls me to sleep. I don't know how long I have been sleeping. When I open my eyes, I find that the car has stopped but we are not at home. We are instead parked outside a one-storey terrace house. Auntie May gets out of the car and, as soon as she has let herself into the house's compound through the gate, Papa drives off. As he does so, he glances at me through the rearview mirror and sees that I am awake. "When we get home, don't tell Mama about Auntie May, okay?" I want to ask why but Papa has a stern look on his face and I dare not, so I just nod my head. "And if Mama asks why you are late coming home, tell her that you had a school activity and you had forgotten to tell her about it." I nod again, wondering why he wants me to lie.

It is evening when we reach home. I can see that the lights of our bungalow house are on as Papa parks the car under the porch. The front door opens before he has switched off the car engine, and Mama comes out. She must be worried, wondering why I wasn't back home from school. As Papa and I are about to get out of the car, he gives me a look and I remember the lie that I must tell Mama.

Of course, Mama isn't happy at all that I hadn't told her about the so-called school activity. "I've been worried sick thinking about what could have happened to you," she scolds. Papa also gets a scolding, "I called your office but your secretary said you were out since morning." I look at Papa as he shrugs his shoulders, "I had some outside work." Mama turns her attention back to me, "Don't do this to me again, okay? I almost called the police. Now, go and take your bath. We are having dinner soon."

As we eat dinner together, Papa and Mama talk to one another as they usually do, and Mama hasn't any idea at all about what actually happened. Mama is no longer angry and is enjoying his stories and jokes. But I eat quietly. I don't like having to lie to Mama and I can't help but feel angry at Papa for making me feel so strange. I may only be twelve years old but I'm not stupid. There must be a reason why I have to lie to Mama and that reason has something to do with Auntie May.

"Are you sick?" Mama looks at me in a concerned way and puts the back of her left hand on my forehead. "You're very quiet." Papa gets up to wash his hands, "She must be tired. She has had a busy day." Mama gets up as well. "You'd better go to sleep early and have a good rest," she tells me. Papa keeps his eyes on me as I leave the table, wash my hands and go upstairs to my bedroom.

I try to go to sleep but as soon as I close my eyes, I see Auntie May in my mind. Who is she? Why can't I tell Mama about her? The questions give me a headache and I think that it would be good if I do get sick and not have to go to school tomorrow. Who knows? If I were to go to school, Auntie May could be with Papa when he comes to pick me up after school and what do I do then? Would I have to lie to Mama again?

It has been weeks and there has been no Auntie May in Papa's car. Papa has not said anything about her to me and it is as if I have never met her. I am, naturally, curious about her but Papa doesn't look like he wants to say anything. Papa has never been one to tell me things; it is Mama who keeps me informed about plans for the family, what we are to do over the weekend, where we will be going for our holiday. People have told me that Papa is reserved and doesn't talk much. Which is true; whenever Grandpa, Mama's father, comes to visit for a few days, he and Papa can sit in the living room together for hours and not say much to one another. But then again, when his friends come by, Papa is not reserved at all and is often the most talkative in the group. So Papa does have many sides to him and I wonder how he is with Auntie May; is he reserved or talkative with her?

It is a Saturday afternoon and Mama and I are at home. Papa has gone out with his friends. Mama is busy with her embroidery, something that I'm not particularly interested in. I prefer to curl up with a book rather than tediously stab a needle into a drawing on a piece of cotton material. We are both in the living room, she sitting in an armchair and me lying prone on the floor, my chin cupped in my palms as I read the book opened in front of me. She glances at me and says, "You really should sit up properly when you read. You will spoil your eyesight reading like that." I don't reply but carried on with my reading.

She continues to look at me; something seems to be on her mind. From the corner of my eye, I can see her mouth opening as if she wants to talk to me but she closes it, shakes her head and turns her attention back to her embroidery. Mama is a very correct person who gives a lot of thought to what she says or does. And I am constantly taught about how to behave in the company of other people, making me one very polite young person. That's what her friends say when they meet me, "My goodness, she is so courteous for her age."

Presently, Mama puts down her embroidery and tells me to take a bath and get dressed. "Papa will be home soon," she says. "We're going out for dinner, remember? Make sure you wear something suitable. We're going to a Chinese restaurant." Papa and Mama like eating out, and they both particularly like Chinese food. I do too and have surprised many with my adeptness in eating with chopsticks.

We arrive at the restaurant, where Papa has obviously reserved a special table, because the waitress leads us towards a room along one side of the dining area. She pushes back the sliding door, we enter the room and I am shocked to find Auntie May already seated at the table. With her is a boy who looks like he's about ten years old. I don't know what to do or say. Shall I pretend that I haven't met her before? If it looks like I know her, Mama will wonder why and will find out about the lie I told her so many weeks ago.

Auntie May gets up as we enter the room. If Mama is surprised about our dinner guests, she is not showing it and she waits for Papa to introduce Auntie May to her. They *salam* one another and Auntie May then looks at me and I *salam* her, not saying anything. I feel grateful that she has not given any indication that we have met before. She then puts her hand on the boy's shoulders, "This is Kassim", and Kassim gets up and *salam* Papa and Mama. We all sit down and Papa must have pre-ordered the food, as it doesn't take long before the waitress comes into the room with a big bowl of shark's fin soup. I eat and listen to the adults talking, and they talk as if Kassim and I are not in the room.

"May called me some weeks ago," Papa is telling Mama. "That's how I found out that Yem had married her without Jah's knowledge. May is still married to Yem, this boy is their son. She came to me because Yem has been neglecting her and the boy." Yem is Papa's older brother and Jah is his wife.

"Oh dear, my husband told me that there's a family problem relating to Yem but I didn't know that it is this complicated," Mama says to Auntie May. "But what do you want us to do? This is a family thing, between Yem, Jah and you. I don't think we can get involved, especially since Jah doesn't even know. She is my closest sister-in-law and I don't want her to get hurt by this."

Auntie May shakes her head. "I don't want anyone to get hurt. But I have my rights too as Yem's second wife. He can't just let us be. I haven't seen him for months. Fortunately, I have a job. Otherwise, Kassim and I won't have a roof over our heads. I pay for everything, the house, our food. But Yem is my husband and he is obligated to support us." Kassim looks at Auntie May at the mention of his name, and I wonder if he understands what's being said. As for me, I may be twelve but I'm not stupid. Auntie May continues, "All I'm asking is that you remind him of his obligations towards Kassim and me. If he doesn't want to see us again, he should at least divorce me."

"I think we have no choice but to help," Papa says to both Auntie May and Mama. "Yem is doing a lot of wrong here, first by marrying without Jah's knowledge, then by pretending that he hasn't a second family and, even worse, neglecting this second family. Knowing all this, we can't just keep quiet about it. We will be in complicity with him if we don't do something." Auntie May looks at Papa with relief and Mama nods her head in agreement. "You'll have to advise him," she tells Papa.

After our pancake dessert, Papa pays the bill and we all get up. As Auntie May and Kassim had come to the restaurant in a taxi, Papa offers them a lift back to their house. Everyone is quiet during the drive. When we reach the house, Auntie May opens the rear door but before she steps out of the car, she thanks Papa and Mama for the dinner and their willingness to help her. She then looks to me, "I didn't invite you into my house the last time. It's late now so I can't invite you in this time. You must come again and get to know Kassim better."

Mama turns her head in my direction and one of her eyebrows is lifted in a question-mark.

Shopping can be Hazardous

by James Ooi

I am writing this because I am asked to do this. And in thirty minutes. So I'll just write about last week's class where we were asked to go to the nearby mall to talk to someone there and write about it. Raman, my writing class instructor suggested that the class do it as a creative writing project.

Ok lah, he's the boss so here goes.

Damn! It was a hot afternoon. Just walking out of the bookshop and onto the road, I could feel the blistering heat. My hand and arms felt like it was sizzling onto the grill being barbequed to a crisp. Hurriedly, I strode along the weather beaten road and into the cool air conditioning of the mall.

So I had to find someone to talk with. Yeah, hopefully some hot girl is gonna respond to my advances. Or I might get a slap and have to turn back in to class with a red face. I could probably say it's sunburn or something.

Or I could chat up a guy and get punched in the face for propositioning him. Maybe I should send Raman the medical bill for getting us to do this zany exercise. Okay, okay. I'll look for the first gay guy I see and just chat him up. This way I won't get slapped or punched in the face but I'd probably get molested instead, I guess.

Walking along the busy and cluttered upper ground floor, I chanced upon this rustic and ambient arty-farty shop selling some earthen pots with water flowing out of them. Yeah, what a rip-off. RM800 for an urn and water flowing out of it. I could probably buy the same stuff at the local pasar malam.

But still, the shop was nicely decorated and it had a warm rustic feeling to it. You have some statues of Buddha around, a couple of beautifully painted artwork of Buddha's head. I almost bought the painting. And the shop owner, who was gay, was a very handsome guy who came over and started telling me in a very fascinating manner about his shop.

Let's call him Gary. Gary's a clean-cut guy, handsome in the guy-next-door kinda manner, nice short-cropped hair and a smile that girls would probably swoon over. But he is gay. How the heck do I know? I know, I just know he's gay.

I guess even though he wasn't exactly the feminine type but he has some unmistakable mannerisms that actually made me realize that he was one of them. My cousin's gay so I know how to recognize one. Especially after the incident one night of drunken partying at Rum Jungle when this long time friend of mine just grabbed me and gave it straight to me on the lips with some tongue action man! That was so sick that I puked and I washed my mouth with Listerine over and over again when I got back.

Gary had a very interesting manner in the way he spoke. You kinda felt that he was paying attention to you and you alone. It was very hypnotizing and I didn't feel much of a regret as I parted with about a hundred ringgit for some souvenirs.

Suddenly, he said to me conspiratorially, "Say, I just have this feeling that I want to share something with you. It's about your future."

Incredulously, I joked, "What?? I just parted with a hundred ringgit buying stuff from you. You want me to place a standing order for strange Thai artifacts from your shop every month issit?"

Gary laughed, "No, nothing like that. I have some skills in tarot reading. I just felt led to do a reading for you."

Intrigued, I said, "Ok cool. Let's do it."

Sitting at his table, he passed me a deck of cards and told me to shuffle them. I shuffled them and handed it back to him. Gary cut the deck, split the deck into three piles and put the lowest pile back on top of the other two. I was then asked to select 9-cards from the shuffled deck.

Placing a 9-card spread onto the table, Gary said in a low mysterious tone, "The first three cards represent the past, the next three - the present and the last three - the future."

"Looking at the past, I see that you have had many relationships which have started well but ultimately ended as just friends. I also see that you have had 5 serious relationships. It seems to me that you have yet to find the soul mate in your past life."

Impressed I said, "Amazing. That's absolutely true. How do you do that?"

"The present cards tells me that you are now searching for that someone new. And the future tells me that you will find that someone but it will be something that you will not expect it to be."

"Do you believe in reincarnation?"

I replied, "Yes, I do."

Gary grasped my right hand and gazed directly into my eyes, "I have this revelation that I feel I want to tell you but I don't know if I should. How would you want me to do this? It might be traumatic for you, you know."

Feeling more curious and even a bit suspenseful, I said, "Tell me lah. After all, you have gone too far to stop now."

Then Gary smiled suggestively to me, "What I am telling you now may surprise you. I am your wife from your previous life. You and I are meant to be together in this life."

4. *Shopping can be Hazardous by James Ooi*

I am writing this because I am asked to do this. And in thirty minutes. So I'll just write about last week's class where we were asked to go to the nearby mall to talk to someone there and write about it. Raman, my writing class instructor suggested that the class do it as a creative writing project.

Ok lah, he's the boss so here goes.

Damn! It was a hot afternoon. Just walking out of the bookshop and onto the road, I could feel the blistering heat. My hand and arms felt like it was sizzling onto the grill being barbequed to a crisp. Hurriedly, I strode along the weather beaten road and into the cool air conditioning of the mall.

So I had to find someone to talk with. Yeah, hopefully some hot girl is gonna respond to my advances. Or I might get a slap and have to turn back in to class with a red face. I could probably say it's sunburn or something.

Or I could chat up a guy and get punched in the face for propositioning him. Maybe I should send Raman the medical bill for getting us to do this zany exercise. Okay, okay. I'll look for the first gay guy I see and just chat him up. This way I won't get slapped or punched in the face but I'd probably get molested instead, I guess.

Walking along the busy and cluttered upper ground floor, I chanced upon this rustic and ambient arty-farty shop selling some earthen pots with water flowing out of them. Yeah, what a rip-off. RM800 for an urn and water flowing out of it. I could probably buy the same stuff at the local pasar malam.

But still, the shop was nicely decorated and it had a warm rustic feeling to it. You have some statues of Buddha around, a couple of beautifully painted artwork of Buddha's head. I almost bought the painting. And the shop owner, who was gay, was a very handsome guy who came over and started telling me in a very fascinating manner about his shop.

Let's call him Gary. Gary's a clean-cut guy, handsome in the guy-next-door kinda manner, nice short-cropped hair and a smile that girls would probably swoon over. But he is gay. How the heck do I know? I know, I just know he's gay.

I guess even though he wasn't exactly the feminine type but he has some unmistakable mannerisms that actually made me realize that he was one of them. My cousin's gay so I know how to recognize one. Especially after the incident one night of drunken partying at Rum Jungle when this long time friend of mine just grabbed me and gave it straight to me on the lips with some tongue action man! That was so sick that I puked and I washed my mouth with Listerine over and over again when I got back.

Gary had a very interesting manner in the way he spoke. You kinda felt that he was paying attention to you and you alone. It was very hypnotizing and I didn't feel much of a regret as I parted with about a hundred ringgit for some souvenirs.

Suddenly, he said to me conspiratorially, "Say, I just have this feeling that I want to share something with you. It's about your future."

Incredulously, I joked, "What?? I just parted with a hundred ringgit buying stuff from you. You want me to place a standing order for strange Thai artifacts from your shop every month issit?"

Gary laughed, "No, nothing like that. I have some skills in tarot reading. I just felt led to do a reading for you."

Intrigued, I said, "Ok cool. Let's do it."

Sitting at his table, he passed me a deck of cards and told me to shuffle them. I shuffled them and handed it back to him. Gary cut the deck, split the deck into three piles and put the lowest pile back on top of the other two. I was then asked to select 9-cards from the shuffled deck.

Placing a 9-card spread onto the table, Gary said in a low mysterious tone, "The first three cards represent the past, the next three - the present and the last three - the future."

"Looking at the past, I see that you have had many relationships which have started well but ultimately ended as just friends. I also see that you have had 5 serious relationships. It seems to me that you have yet to find the soul mate in your past life."

Impressed I said, "Amazing. That's absolutely true. How do you do that?"

"The present cards tells me that you are now searching for that someone new. And the future tells me that you will find that someone but it will be something that you will not expect it to be."

"Do you believe in reincarnation?"

I replied, "Yes, I do."

Gary grasped my right hand and gazed directly into my eyes, "I have this revelation that I feel I want to tell you but I don't know if I should. How would you want me to do this? It might be traumatic for you, you know."

Feeling more curious and even a bit suspenseful, I said, "Tell me lah. After all, you have gone too far to stop now."

Then Gary smiled suggestively to me, "What I am telling you now may surprise you. I am your wife from your previous life. You and I are meant to be together in this life."

5. THE PLAN.doc by Kow Shih-Li

Tuesday

Today, I am at the bank, as always. The fluorescent lights throw a flat, white brightness on everything including the plastic potted palm standing by the grey blinds. Everything is sterile and inorganic, including me in my starched, white shirt. The continual whirring of the bubble jet printer is unrelenting, printer-head grinding its teeth on accordion-folded, four-ply paper. I am as accustomed to this background noise as I am to the sound of my own breathing but today, its dogged busyness jars my senses. The inescapable dreariness of mechanical efficiency is distressing.

I have been sleepless for three nights now. Some non-existent pump in my gut is pushing adrenalin through my body. Continually nervous, I feel as though I am standing on metal grating in a high place through which I can see the long fall down. Maybe it's the tea-lady's coffee, maybe it's Her.

Work is a distraction. My shirt collar chafes the back of my neck, the tie presses against my throat like the cliched noose. I have to plan for bigger things now. I have to plan for Her. It is impossible to concentrate. The dotted lines awaiting my signature float in and out of my field of vision randomly as I try to focus on the loan approval forms. Fuad had better be diligent checking though the paperwork.

Wednesday

I am told I have an analytical mind. A way with numbers, never misses details yet always sees the big picture. The powers that be tell me that in my annual performance appraisals every year, without fail. Of course I have a bloody analytical mind. What other kind of mind would a dean's list accounting student with a Masters in International Finance have, the morons?

Today, this exemplary mind is taxed by the thoughts of Her and lunch last Saturday. It was Japanese, always safe for a first date. No sharing of food, no clumsy cutting, no splattering gravy, no messy servings and prawn shells strewn on table cloths wet by tea. Only convenient, bite sized pieces on individual plates that you could transport into your mouth without appearing undignified.

So, we ate, sitting across each other at a small table, a young couple on the other side of the fake rice paper screen. Conversation ebbed and flowed with the tea. Her hands were beautiful, curled around the glazed teacup. She smiled a lot and laughed a little. She would be away, she said, for a few days.

Would I call her when she got back?

Thursday

The framed poster in my office proclaims, "A dream is just a dream. A goal is a dream with a plan and a deadline. -Harvey Mackay-" I did not know who this Mackay was but plan I shall.

It has been 5 days since we first met. I could not remember her face, only the fact that it was pleasing enough. The prospect of seeing her again tomorrow excites me. I plan an agenda for the next two months. Ten dates tabled under the headers Date, Meal Type, Restaurant Options and Other Activity. I had vicarious pleasure with Other Activity. Date-plan.doc is saved in my Personal Folder on the computer.

Friday - The Second Date

Her favourite steak place was a dimly lit colonial bungalow. In the candle-illumined gloominess, we talked about work. Listening to her voice lilting around narrations of difficult clients and the tiredness of being on the road, I drank 2 beers and felt the nervous anticipation of the week drain away from the base of my spine. She had red wine with her medium rare. God, I love a woman who eats red meat. When we finished, she touched my arm with her beautiful hand as she got up from her chair. A fleeting two seconds, a slight pressure burning a hole through my sleeve. I thought she was heaven sent and hot as hell.

Monday

The bank has me in its confines again. Lee Mei, my assistant, is driving me crazy with her rational explanations of why every problem she brought to me had a right to exist and was impossible to solve. Fuad has been sensible enough to stay away and feign independence. The slowness of time makes me increasingly crabby.

I type out an imaginary conversation with Her, save it as Conv-plan.doc and mark as 'Done' Date No. 2 in my dating schedule.

Tuesday - The Third Date

I had an Other Activity planned; an artsy Chinese movie with subtitles. Her closeness in the darkness of the cinema was discomforting, the space between our shoulders hung like a tangible mass. The movie was filled with grandly coloured scenes but I barely heard the dialogue. I was too busy rehearsing, in my head, the witty conversation that I had concocted yesterday. I would use that over teh tarik and thosai after the movie.

It worked brilliantly. I brimmed with charm and she was adorable in her compliance to my scheme to win her.

Wednesday

She calls and we speak on the phone in the privacy of my office for twenty-five minutes. I spend another forty-five replaying the conversation in my head, reinterpreting for clues. Someone less pragmatic would have called the analyzing cold-blooded; I prefer to think that I am searching for a way into her beautiful mind.

Two cursory knocks on my open door. "Good morning, Andrew. Where's that monthly loan status report you were supposed to give me yesterday?" I am startled but the matronly bulk of Mrs Tan is already lowering itself into my visitor chair. Chain-smoking, audit tyrant from HQ. I didn't know she was at the branch today. Shit.

"Hey, Mrs Tan. I didn't know you were coming today. Fuad! Somebody, get Fuad please and tell him to bring the loan status report."

Mrs Tan lights a cigarette. That woman has no decorum at all, and it is against branch regulations to smoke indoors. My coffee cup turns into an ashtray. I hated her stubby fingers. They were so inelegant compared to Hers.

"Come on, Andrew. You're slipping up. You always meet your deadlines and now you've missed three in 2 weeks. This is not going to look good in your appraisal. What's wrong? You lovesick or what?" she said, emphasizing 'not' with a little pause and puff of smoke.

"No'lah, Mrs Tan. Everyone is just a little overstretched. That new loan scheme HQ launched last week is flying and we're just trying to cope with the response. I haven't had a good break since I don't know when."

"Is that so? Well, maybe you should take some time off when you sort out this mess." She steals a glance at my computer screen. Thank god I had just opened a busy looking Excel file to work on.

Fuad comes in with the loan status report, looking mousy in a beige shirt. Mrs Tan is diverted, she has fresh prey.

Saturday - The Fourth Date

It went exactly as planned. We spent the whole day together. Shopping, eating, another movie. Her closeness was no longer a thing to be conscious of. We held hands and it was perfectly natural.

Over dinner, I told her about Mrs Tan and the people at work, making Mrs Tan uglier and the rest more incompetent than they actually were. It threw my own competencies into clearer relief, I thought. She laughed, said "You're so mean" and slapped me on the arm. What would I say to my friends about her? I told her and she fell silent.

Sunday - The Fifth Date

The walk back to the car from the restaurant was secluded. I kissed her and she leaned in.

It was a triumph of planning and execution. The Kiss was 2 dates ahead of schedule.

I allowed myself to think about a future involving a diamond ring of a certain size. This was The Big Picture.

*****

I stopped planning dates because there was no longer a need. We were calling each other several times a day, and meeting as often as we could. I started planning a little holiday away. A 3-day rendezvous at the beach, probably Langkawi. I booked the AirAsia tickets from the office and filled out an Annual Leave Application form.

The people in the office say I look good. I agree. A spring in my step, a sparkle in my eye. Work was no longer a burden. In fact, I excelled - I was incisive, emphatic, even warm and connected. Fuad and Lee Mei flourished under my effectiveness. Mrs Tan would have no reason to visit again.

Food tasted better.

The Holiday

She was surprised when I told her about Langkawi. Not as happy as I expected she would be but she said was tired from the pressure of meeting quotas. The month was coming to an end and she had to sell more insurance policies to make her numbers.

"Why don't you sell me a policy? How short are you on your quota?"

"I couldn't. It's not right. This is too personal, you can't bail me out all the time."

"Why not? Anyway, I don't have one of those medical cum life cum unit trust type of fancy schemes you have. "

The monthly premiums could have paid for a small car but what the heck. She would love me for it. I was doing well at work and my transfer to HQ would come through in 6 months.

In Langkawi, I gave her a necklace with a little diamond heart. Just to let you know you're special. Oh, I love you, she said, with tears in her eyes. The sun set behind her, an orange globe swallowed by the single line of the horizon. I had a right to be smug. It was perfectly timed, perfectly planned. The sky flushed a rosy pink. All was right with my

*****

I had another preoccupation now. Planning a marriage and a new life after. I was filling in the colours of The Big Picture.

The structured demands of a HQ career worked well for me. My name cards have been reprinted twice, each time with a title bearing more letters and hyphens. A real plant with juicy, verdant leaves sits next to my office door. There are no printers within earshot. Bliss.

An October wedding would be ideal. We'd have Christmas together for a honeymoon and be comfortably acclimatized to face Chinese New Year in January as an angpow-giving couple together.

The Proposal

I made reservations at an expensive French restaurant. A resident four-piece string quartet would provide a suitably romantic ambience, I was told.

The half-carat ring is in my pocket. I had taken care to wear dark trousers so that I would not have a stain on them after I got up from bended knee. The menu would be light and delicate. Salads, pates, fish, soufflé, wine, mousse.

On the way to dinner, she disgorged the daily complaints about work and her boss. It was tiresome to listen to but it was her routine. I let it wash over me. It would be another coup; I had the perfect evening planned. She would say yes, the strings would play and I would be on my way to a perfect, married life.

After the cheese and before the dessert, the quartet moved close. It turned out to be a Filipino mariachi group, all grinning broadly. What the heck. The only strings were the six on the guitar. The bongo playe had the drums hanging

down to his shins. I pushed my chair back. I have something to ask you. Down on one knee, smoothly practised.

"Will you marry me?" Ring box clacked open decisively, the diamond was a triumphant, multi pointed sparkling star.

She had a strange smile on her face. It looked almost pained. I noticed then that she wasn't dressed her best. It must have been a rough working day. I didn't remember what she had said in the car. Her shoes had a ring of dried mud around the soles and her make-up had lost definition.

"No."

The word quivered in the air. I saw us frozen as in a still photograph. She in her chair, me in the ludicrous pose, the guitar, the bongos, the tambourine and the maracas in attendance. The 'No' written in thick strokes hanging over our heads.

The music faltered, leaving the singer unaccompanied for an awkward second, his voice unadorned. He wavered, picked up the song again and started to walk to another table. The rest followed the cue. My chair felt like it was a million miles away.

Dessert arrived, chocolate mousse with strawberries and sugar dusting in the shape of a heart. It all seemed so contrived now, like a Valentine's Day gimmick.

"Why?"

"Because…because this has all been about you and only you. You don't know me. I am not an acquisition merger joint venture whatever. What am I all about? What did I dream of today? What do I want? I am not a scheduled timetable to be followed and executed. Not a target to be met, to help you achieve a goal of marriage before you turn 40. I am not incidental. I refuse to be."

Quietly aflame, her tone was low and her face controlled but I did not see her. My excellent and reliable mind was already reacting, making a list of counteractions to deal with this. Plans for finding a substitute, for apologising, for trying again, raced through my consciousness. The logic machine was moving in full gear. Yet I could almost, almost but not quite see, like a speck of dirt on my glasses that wants to be ignored, something in there crumbling like a house of cards. That speck, in its quietness, knew that something would break and would not heal but I do not accept that. Planning and effort conquers all. There would be no failure. Grief was not permitted.

"And happy birthday, by the way. It's next week isn't it? Turning 40 isn't so bad," she said.

She got up to leave, putting both her beautiful hands on the table. When she was gone, the Langkawi heart was left on the table where her hands were. Small and encrusted in glassy stone.

I tried to drink, swallowing was painful. Breathing hurt but all I needed was another Plan. Mr Maracas' curious eye was set on me, he was singing back up. Bloody musicians